From A Different View

A collection of short stories and verse inspired by the local landscape taking a journey around mid Wales to look at life and death from an unusual perspective.

by
Kate Coldham

illustrations by
Nick Coldham

for Nick & Adelaide — *believing in yourself is always easier when someone else believes in you first.*

First published 2011

ISBN 978-1-4475-3320-7

Copyright © Kate Coldham 2011

The right of Kate Coldham to be identified as the author of this work has been asserted by her in accordance with the Copyright, Designs and Patents Act 1988.

Copyright © Nick Coldham 2011

All illustrations within this publication are the property Nick Coldham in accordance with the Copyright, Designs and Patents Act 1988.

To view or purchase more art work visit Nick Coldham's website on:

www.tan-y-coed.co.uk

All rights reserved. No part of this publication may be reproduced, stored in or introduced into a retrieval system, or transmitted, in any form, or by means (electronic, mechanical, photocopying, recording or otherwise) without the prior written permission of the author. Any person who does any unauthorised act in relation to this publication may be liable to criminal prosecution and civil claims for damages.

From A Different View

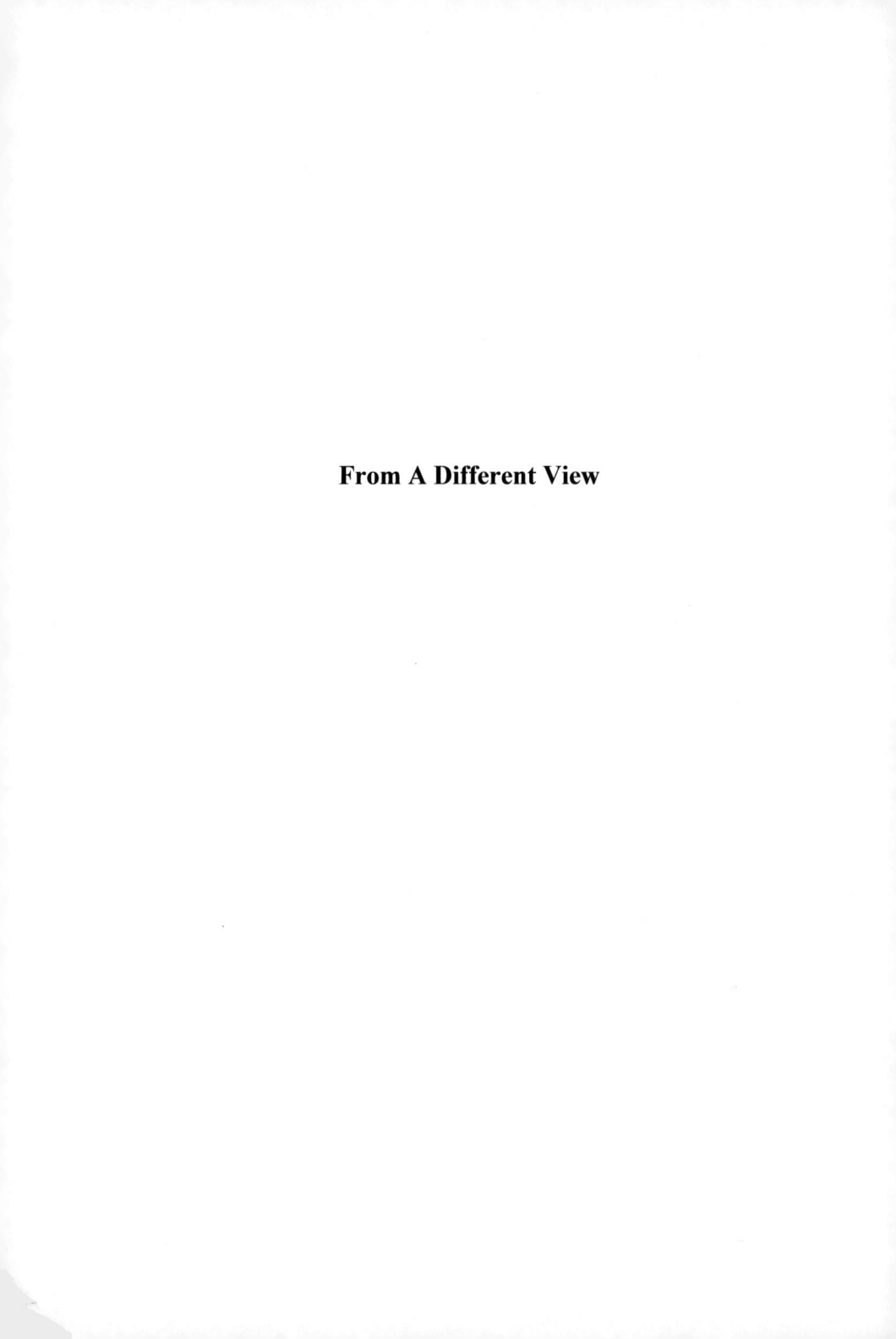

Contents

The House	9
Intensive Care	17
'Til Death us do Part	27
Be Careful What You Wish For	33
Don't Tell Me It's Over	41
The Bird and the Beast	47
Waiting to Die	51
Spirits of the Sky	59
The Nine Lives of Kitty Carter	63
Time	68

The House

I wrote this is because someone very close to me always pointed out this place as we drove to Newtown, and said how she felt it was a house that deserved having a story written about it. I am not entirely sure, however, that this was the type of story she had in mind...

* * * * *

There is this house, just outside the village of Caersws. You can see it quite clearly sometimes, particularly during the late autumn, when the leaves are piled high up in dry heaps along the hedgerows leaving the tree branches bare, like old scrawny arms clutching at the ever darkening clouds. If you drive along the road to Y Drenewydd, it stands out on the hillside above the low mist like a giant striped humbug, its stark half-timbered face seeming somehow out of place against the rolling countryside.

If you want a closer look, you have to navigate your way along the spider's web of country lanes that criss-cross the valley. Go past a couple of slightly run down farms and through an old wood, until, unexpectedly, it will loom darkly on your left, grand and imposing, and yet with an air of resigned sadness about it. The once grand Elizabethan windows, with their myriad of cracked and age coloured panes glint back at you in the half-light that filters through the trees, and the low wooden door, its ornate carvings worn with weather, seems impenetrably locked forever.

I must have passed it hundreds of times without paying it any attention, always focused on the way ahead, the day ahead. But then, without warning, something makes me look up, makes me see it for the first time, and now, as I continue my eternal search along this route, I find my eyes automatically scanning the green fields for its black and white façade, rewarded by the sudden glimpse of it as I reach a break in the hedgerows. I always feel a strange comfort in its centuries old consistency, and it seems to somehow sooth my restless soul.

It is a wet autumn day that I finally leave my normal path and begin to seek out a closer look at the house along the leafy lanes. Eventually, I find myself standing outside, staring at the crumbling brick work. Close up, you can really begin to imagine its original beauty. There remain some traces of the decorative cornices, and although the paint has long since peeled from the rotting wood, you can still admire the craftsmanship. The roof, too, is in bad need of repair, and I am sure that it won't be long before the ivy, that has begun to creep up the walls like an infectious disease, will spread its curious fingers under the slate tiles and worm its way inside.

My curiosity is aroused, and, distracted from my normal routine, I begin to research the history of the house, intrigued that its owner would allow it to slowly die like this, lost and forgotten. But unlocking the secrets of the house is proving difficult. I sometimes watch the Estate Agents shake their heads with regret, agreeing with young couples who are making inquiries about the place that it would indeed be a great purchase but that, as far as they know, it has been in the same family for centuries. I can tell that any hope they have of getting their hands on a nice fat commission has long since faded. The local farmers are less willing to discuss the place, shaking their heads and feigning ignorance with any curious passer-by, and commonly resorting to open hostility, standing defensively behind their barking dogs if I get too close.

Increasingly, I find myself thinking about the house, intrigued and frustrated by its hidden mystery, and more and more, I am leaving my search on that road to Y Drenewydd, creating excuses in my head so that I can wander up to the house to stop and stare almost imploringly at the walls, as if the house itself could somehow open up and tell me its story.

I have almost decided to give up, to return to my usual routine when I have an idea that I should try the local newspapers. In the back of my mind I recall a rumour that something might have happened at the house, some incident that caused a bit of local excitement for a brief spell, and so, in spite of the daunting prospect of trawling through years of records, I embark on my investigations with renewed vigour.

It takes a few weeks of searching but I am determined. At last I find something, tucked away in the centre pages of a yellowed issue of the Cambrian News. I scan the words eagerly, and find myself amused by the reporter's obvious scepticism. He concludes that the rumours of the house being haunted are over exaggerated, that the supposed reports of footsteps that can be heard echoing along the wooden hallways are merely the result of an over-active imagination. And the fact that the owner no longer lives there is purely because he has work commitments abroad, not because he had been awoken from his sleep too many times by the sound of something heavy being dragged along the floor in the early hours of the morning. The article goes on to describe the details of a previous incident that the house is rumoured to be linked to, but I feel I have learnt enough, and stop reading. Surreptitiously folding the fragile paper and hiding it in my pocket, I leave.

The knowledge that the house is currently empty is all I need to spur me on, although now that I am actually here, I still approach the house with caution, and warily press my face near the glass, squinting into the semi darkness for any sign of movement. Everything is quiet, and the first traces of the setting sun make the window panes glow like a fire. Weeds have long since taken over the ground around the threshold and the door is stiff and unyielding, the hinges rusted. But I am determined and now, after a brief struggle, I am at last inside.

A lifetime of dust has settled on every surface and the ageing timber creaks in protest as I slowly move through the empty rooms, a strange sense of de ja vu flitting through my mind. A mouse, undeterred by my presence, scuttles across the floorboards leaving a faint scattering of paw prints as it disappears under a broken door frame. There is a lingering musty smell of stagnant air, and I find myself shivering at the sudden chill. It is probably my imagination getting the better of me, because I feel the hairs on the back of my neck prickling, and I turn suddenly, half expecting someone to be standing behind me. But unsurprisingly, I am still alone, and I laugh aloud at my flight of fancy, stopping abruptly as the noise of my laughter echoes back at me, incongruous in the tomb like stillness of the house.

A sound upstairs makes me start. To my over active imagination it could sound like footsteps on a wooden floor above me, and I am reminded of the newspaper article. I force myself to adopt the same scepticism as the reporter, telling myself it is just the wood drying out, or perhaps a family of squirrels nesting in the roof, then I hurry to the staircase, suddenly eager to finish my explorations and leave this place. The stairs are broad, and each one worn down into a smooth curve in the centre. I am reluctant to disturb the cobwebs stretched out on the banister, but I feel unsteady, and need the support. The sticky grey strands wrap around my fingers, and when I reach the top, I try to shake them off. That is when I notice it. In the fading light, I can see two thick lines in the dust on the floor, shaky and uneven in places, but unmistakeable. The remaining traces that a body has been dragged along the hallway. That is when I know for certain I have been here before.

Almost in disbelief at this unexpected ending to my age long search, I cautiously follow the trail to the end of the corridor until it disappears under the skirting board into the wood panelled wall. I am excited by my discovery, and quickly pulling the newspaper from my bag, I move closer to a window to scan the remaining lines, to confirm what I have now realised. All that time spent travelling up and down that main road, all those fruitless years of looking only to find that it is here, in this house, that I would finally get my answers. The greying print is just visible as I take in the words that have been written about the case. It confirms that although the police had searched all around here all those years ago, to try and find a body, they had remained unsuccessful. They had even at one point reluctantly examined this house, quickly dismissing the rumours that the ghostly noises were proof of a murder. But they hadn't known to look behind this panelling, and so they hadn't discovered the secret room hidden at the end of this hallway. And so, when their search had ended a few months later, the case remained unsolved.

My hand automatically reaches out to touch the wood and it feels smooth and warm against my fingertips. I picture the dry white bones of the skeleton concealed behind it in its silent tomb, and imagine its stick like fingers reaching back towards me, mirroring my actions, finally reconnecting body and soul after an age of searching, a lifetime of waiting. It could be worse, I think to myself with a wry smile, that this isn't all that bad a place to be, that there are worse graves for your body to be hidden in for eternity. After all, given the circumstances of my disappearance, I could have easily found myself buried under a pile of cold rotting leaf mulch deep in the forest, food for passing foxes and eventually the worms. At least here it is dry, if only until the house loses its constant battle against the ever persistent onslaught of nature. And maybe soon, the owner will return, or perhaps sell the house on to someone who will turn it back into a home, someone who doesn't mind the fact there is a ghost here. That I am here.

As I said before, there is this house, hiding amongst the bare branches, waiting silently in the centre of its web of hedgerow lined lanes. The windows, like cataract occluded eyes, still watch the outside world sadly, and reflect the grey clouds that drift above. It is a house waiting to be rediscovered, but it is a house with a secret, although I now know that secret, because I am that secret. You should come and visit sometime. Take a detour off the main road to Y Drenewydd and wind your way up to the woods. And if you have time, step out of your car for a while and take a look round. There are a few more broken panes now, and you will need to watch out that a tile doesn't slip from the roof above you. The weather has worn away most of the original carvings and the weeds completely cover the front path, because no one ever calls here anymore, but if you are persistent, you can still get up close. You might even choose to peer in through the dusty windows, although I doubt you will see anything.

And the old wooden front door? Well that, at least for me, is now inescapably locked forever.

Intensive Care

In spite of the beauty of our local landscapes that pass as you wind your way along our narrow roads, there are still a few visitors who seem to feel that arriving at their destination quickly is more important than appreciating the journey. So next time you think you want to overtake on that blind corner, remember, you never truly know what might be around it...

* * * * *

Treacle. It feels to him like he is lying in thick treacle, because his arms and legs don't really want to respond to the suggestions his brain is making for them to move. He is surprised that he doesn't feel more frustrated by this, but an overwhelming tiredness floods his head, and he allows it to take over, allows it to sink his mind back into the foggy nothingness.

Later, it could just be moments or it could be hours, he is not entirely sure, he can hear a voice, or perhaps it is two, persistently droning in the distance, and almost automatically he thinks about reaching out to turn off what must be the radio. He doesn't remember actually hitting the 'snooze' button, but now the voices have stopped,

and so he assumes in his sleepy state, that he has managed. Just another ten minutes, he reasons, and then he will drag himself out of bed. He starts to calculate how late he can get up and still manage to arrive back at work on time, but his thought process sticks on the endless country lanes that he will have to negotiate before getting back to civilisation. He mentally curses the fact he allowed his wife to persuade him to exchange their usual two week hotel holiday on the continent for this remote bed and breakfast in the Welsh mountains. He is also regretting his decision to drive back to the city early on the Monday morning to avoid the Sunday evening rush hour home.

His car. There is something important he feels he should remember about his car, but he can't quite grasp it. There is an incessant regular bleeping coming from somewhere, interrupting his thoughts. It sounds to him like the alarm to remind him about wearing a seatbelt. He immediately guesses what it is. He must have put his heavy briefcase on the passenger seat beside him again, and the car computer assumes the weight is another person. He keeps meaning to ask the garage about whether that can be switched off somehow. He heaves a sigh and wonders how much longer he has got before the radio comes on again.

"David?"

A voice, although faint, cuts through his train of thought.

"David? Can you hear me?"

The voice is disturbing, and he tries to tune it out, wanting to resume the part of his dream where he is cruising along the winding lanes, empty of all traffic, and in particular slow annoying tractors, enjoying the smooth acceleration as he puts his foot to the floor.

"David?"

He feels his body jolt, and at the same moment, in his thoughts, the steering wheel in his hands twists awkwardly. The images in his head shrink to a pin prick of light as if someone has pulled the plug out of an old fashioned television screen. Already the memories are slipping away and he finds himself grasping for them, certain that there was something he needs to remember. But that radio has come on again, voices murmuring in the background and he begins to try and clear his head, to rouse himself in readiness to begin the day.

The pin prick of light is still there, and so is that bleeping alarm. A moment of panic floods through his body like a shot of adrenaline. Maybe he is not still in bed about to get up for work, maybe he is already on his way. Beside him, something, or is it someone, is in the passenger seat because the seatbelt alarm is still going off. He hasn't got time to figure out why. He is racing a little too fast because there was the inevitable slow lorry struggling to manage the gradient of the mountain pass, and he needs to make up time. If he could just get past it...He hears a sudden bang from outside the car and the steering wheel jerks round. The bleeping noise is getting louder, more persistent.

"David....It's OK. Try to relax."

He can feel his heart pounding and tries to focus on the voice, struggling to block out the images in his head, sensations of spinning, turning - are they imagination or memories? As his breathing slows, he wants to reassure himself that it is just the traces of a nightmare, a subconscious reminder of his wife's obvious disapproval over his latest choice of company car. He knows he is a safe driver, but she will insist on worrying, urging him to slow down...

"David, do you know where you are?"

That voice again. It is puzzling him because he can't quite work out who it is, but somehow he hopes that it will answer his questions, that it will make the bad dreams fade away.

"David...do you know where you are? Do you remember? You've been in a car accident."

He can feel a hand on his, cool and soft. He thinks it belongs to the woman who is talking to him. And there are other hands too, on his forehead, his chest, constantly moving. He focuses more on the physical sensations rather than the words, finding them soothing in their constant activity. He knows she is talking about the accident, but now that seems somehow unimportant, as if, after the initial shock, it has faded into the past like an old dream. Gradually, the hands stop moving over him, and he opens his eyes.

The room seems unnaturally bright, and he squints uncomfortably, trying to make sense of the blurred images before him.

"Welcome back, David."

He can make out the outline of a young woman standing over him and she squeezes his hand as she speaks. His mouth feels too dry, making his lips stick uncomfortably, and his attempts to respond are muffled into a quiet groan.

"Shhh, David. Don't try to talk. Just rest."

He blinks to try and clear his clouded vision and as she comes into focus for a few seconds, he can see she is smiling at him. Her crisp white uniform blends into the lightness of the room making her appear almost disembodied, ethereal. Then weariness overtakes him again, and he closes his eyes, allowing the comfort of sleep to enclose him.

When he wakes again, his eyes flutter open, this time adjusting more quickly to the light bathing the room. It looks like early morning sunlight. She is still there, and he wonders whether he has only been briefly dozing or whether it is another day, and for her, another shift. Her hand still fees cool on his, and he tries to return her smile, managing a weak one that he hopes conveys his gratitude at her comforting presence.

His mind is beginning to clear, and he thinks this means that the drugs he must have been given are beginning to wear off. With a slight frown, he wonders what pain that will reveal, and realises that he has no idea how badly hurt he is after the accident. He feels a fleeting moment of anxiety, and opens his mouth to ask, but she has already anticipated his concerns.

"Don't worry, David. You're fine. Everything is going to be OK."

There is a jumble of confused images racing through his mind. Something important that he is on the verge of remembering. Tell me about the accident, he wants to say, but he still can't form the words properly and her hand is now on his forehead, seemingly brushing away the frightening memories of his accident, the car skidding out of control, until the thoughts are distant, as though he is watching it happen to someone else and not him. He remembers now that he was trying to overtake something slow, that out of nowhere a car was coming towards him, and that he had to swerve. In slow motion, he watches his car as it flips over and rolls onto the embankment, coming to a stop against a tree, and he is surprised at his lack of emotion. He feels calm, almost philosophical. At least no-one was hurt, he tells himself. At least he is OK.

He knows he must have been sleeping again, because when he opens his eyes next, there are two people standing nearby, heads bowed in conversation. The pale sunlight is still filtering into the room through a window he can't see, making their faces glow softly, and seem a little out of focus. They are talking quietly and he concentrates hard to try and hear what they are saying.

"...making very good progress..."

"...I think he will be up and out of here soon..."

Heartened by this news, he experiments with trying to lift his arms, and is pleased to find them much more responsive. At his movement, one of the figures turns towards him and, as she draws close enough for him to focus on her face, he immediately recognises her familiar smile.

"How are you feeling now, David?"

Fine. He thinks about his answer for a moment and realises he should be more surprised. He must have been extremely lucky. People usually suffered dreadful injuries in car accidents, and yet here he is, apparently just about ready to be discharged after only...The question drifts into his brain. How long have I actually been here?

"Long enough, don't you think?" there is humour in her voice as she moves around his bed. "Do you feel up to visitors? There's someone outside who is very anxious to see you."

Sure. That would be nice. He suddenly feels an urgency to see his wife, to apologise for putting her through all the worry. Yes, she will probably tell him off for driving too fast again, maybe even say I told you so, but deep down he knows it is because she loves him, that she will be too relieved that he is OK to stay mad at him for long. And, he thinks sheepishly, I could maybe choose a more sensible car to replace the one I have written off. Something slower, to keep her happy, although not too slow...

The door to his room opens, and a woman approaches his bed tentatively, as if afraid of what she might see, afraid of the reception she might receive.

"Don't stay for too long to begin with." he hears the voice say, "It's going to take a bit of time to get used to it."

The words puzzled him for a moment, and he feels that maybe there is something he should be asking, but then the visitor sits herself down by his bed and grasps his hand.

"David, darling."

Something is not quite right. Although it is familiar, it is not his wife's voice. He blinks a few times to focus properly on the face of his visitor. His mother. Then where...? He can't bring himself to finish the question.

"David...I know this is going to be hard for you to take in." she begins.

No. He doesn't want to hear it. The realisation has hit him like a cold wave, chilling his blood. It can't be true.

"David..." his mother is sounding more anxious now.

He tells himself that he won't listen. If he doesn't hear her say the actual words then it won't be true. It can't be true. He tries to stop himself thinking about his wife, but images flash through his head. What about their future together, the plans they had made?

"I'm sorry David, but you have to accept this." Her voice is firm now, but full of genuine affection, just as he remembers it from his childhood. He wants her to hold him like she did when he was young, to tell him that everything is going to be fine. But he knows she can't, because she hasn't held him like that for years, not since he was seven years old, not since she died. His unfinished question wells up again. Then where...where am I?

"In heaven, David."

'Til Death do us Part

This area, not surprisingly because of its beauty, has more than its fair share of local artists. But do their paintings ever really capture the way that life can make you feel...?

* * * * *

Once upon a time, in an old and crumbling stone cottage near the sea, there lived an artist and his wife. Now, this artist loved the sight of the white lace edged waves as they pounded relentlessly against the sandy beach and he loved the slate grey clouds as they darkened the skies above. Every day, he would sit outside, ignoring the chill of the wind as it blew off the sea, and sketch what he saw, smudging his thick pencils across the paper to recreate the most moody of scenes. And every day he would return to his cottage dissatisfied with his work, casting the sheets aside near the log fire with muttered threats of burning them, swearing never to draw again. But his wife would gather up the pages and see the skill in her husband's pictures. And she would tell him that he only needed to add the passion from his heart to make them truly great. Her words would stir in him a determination to go out the next day, to try again. And because of this, the artist loved his wife most of all.

One cold morning in early Spring, as the wind was howling down the chimney scattering ashes onto the hearth, and the skies were the colour of the slate floor, as the artist made ready to leave the cottage, his sketch books and pencils tucked under his arm, he heard his wife call to him from her chair by the fire, and he turned to her, puzzled. And seeing the pallor of her face, he was greatly troubled.

"I am dying." she told him softly, her breaths shallow and weak. "Please do not go out and draw today, but sit with me here instead."

But the artist was afraid of living his life alone. He loved his wife so dearly that he did not want to lose her. He reasoned with himself, if I go outside and continue my work today, then she will not die, because she will have to be here this evening to look at my work, just as she always is. And so he kissed his wife and promised her that he would do just one more day of drawing, and then sit with her tomorrow.

But when he returned to his cottage that evening, his wife was dead, and in his grief, the artist took up all the pictures he had ever created and tossed them into the flames, watching as the heat curled up the edges of his papers and consumed them into ashes, swearing for the last time never to draw again.

The next day, as the sun rose into the pale sky and sent its rays through the rain spattered windows of the cottage, the artist remained sitting beside the fire, watching the final orange embers weaken. He did not gather up his materials, and did not even glance outside, even though the shafts of sunlight created a myriad of diamonds across the gently lapping waves.

And so it was, that he remained sitting there, long after the ashes had turned cold, oblivious to the cotton white clouds that chased across the bright blue heavens, determined not to see the beauty of the world around him, and never touching the pencils that had stained his fingers for so many years.

Then one warm morning, when the green budded stems of the rhododendron bushes were tapping gently at the window panes, the artist looked out through the glass and saw his wife. She was standing at the edge of their garden overlooking the bay and her long hair was dancing in the cool breeze. As he ran outside, she turned to him sadly, and he could see that she was just a spirit, her hazy form barely masking the wild flowers that grew beyond their fence.

"Why do you no longer draw?" she asked him.

"I do not know how." the artist replied. "Without you to encourage me, I have no heart to put pencil to paper. To me the world is grey and lifeless."

"Do you not see beauty around you? Do you not see the sky and the sea?"

"I only see the landscape as I used to draw it. But now the sky is filled with the heavy dark clouds of my despair and the sea sends relentless steely waves of grief to pound against my broken heart."

"Then you must try to find hope within you, for what you draw on your paper, you will create in your life."

The artist thought over her words and an idea began to form in his mind.

"Do not leave me today." he pleaded, "Sit with me whilst I draw so that I may remember our love and have hope."

And so the artist's wife sat upon a bench in their garden and gazed out over the tranquil ocean, speaking no more until the shadows lengthened, and she heard her husband close his box of pencils.

"Come and see my picture." the artist declared, "it is the greatest work I have ever done, for today I have truly added the passion that is in my heart."

Rising from her seat, she crossed the lawn eagerly to view his work. But when she saw it, she could not speak, for there on the page, instead of the wild landscape, was a perfect portrait of her, sitting in their garden surrounded by the spring flowers.

"I have drawn beauty. I have drawn the thing that is most beautiful to me," he told her, "and by doing so, I have enabled you to stay here with me forever, for did you not say that what I draw on my paper, I will create in my life?"

"This is true," she replied with a sad smile, "You have created me as part of your landscape, and so every day, you will find me sitting here in our garden whilst you draw."

The next morning, the artist rose eagerly with the sun and headed out into his garden, his heart filled with renewed hope. There, as she had promised, sat his wife, gazing once more across the seas. Although she spoke little, her presence gave his drawings a depth to match his love for her. Each day, he would hurry outside to be with her, and each evening, he carried into the cottage a pile pictures of which he was proud. Before long, he found his work sought after by many people. From far and wide they travelled, hearing of the amazing landscapes that seemed almost alive on the paper. And the artist worked willingly, but never did he show anyone the portrait he had made of his wife, for that he kept folded up in his pocket so that he could keep her close to his heart.

As the nights drew in with the approach of autumn, he lit candles into the evening to lengthen the day, and lengthen the time he could spend with his beloved wife. And thus he continued for many years until age brought stiffness to his hands and cloudiness to his eyes so that he could no longer hold a pencil, nor see to draw. Yet still, he sat out all day in the garden, just to be with her, until one day, as the sun's final rays glinted across the ripples of the ocean, he closed his eyes, never to wake again.

And at that moment, his wife crossed the garden to him, and as she placed a kiss upon his cold lips, his spirit rose up and stood beside her, his hands stretched out to take hers.

"At last, we are together again." he smiled, "Let us walk our path to the next world hand in hand."

But his wife simply shook her head. "Although I love you dearly, I cannot go with you, my love." she said sadly, "For when you drew me, you made me a part of this landscape, and here I must stay forever, just like the seas below and the skies above."

And the artist realised that his love for his wife had been selfish, that throughout his life he had thought only of his own hopes and fears, caring more for the world he could draw on paper than the real one around him. And because of this, he realised he had created for himself a world without true love.

Be Careful What You Wish For

I was at the local vet with our rabbit for his annual vaccinations and there were three dogs in the waiting room. I found it quite amusing that it was the smallest dog there that made the most noise and demanded the most attention from its owner...

* * * * *

Sitting in the waiting room at the vets, too young to realise that these visits weren't usually fun, were three mongrel puppies. The first, his stocky frame already beginning to show the traces of German shepherd in his blood, the second, with the long legs of a greyhound that were somehow too awkward and gangly, and the third, a small hairy thing that seemed slightly too scruffy to be a Chihuahua. While they waited their turn, they watched the people who walked by the window, passing comments on the sort of dogs they thought these people might choose. Inevitably, their conversation turned boastfully to the lives they dreamed were ahead of them.

"I reckon eventually I'll be an important police dog." began the German shepherd cross. "My great great grandfather was a top guard dog. He protected some really valuable stuff – famous pictures in an art gallery, according to my mum. She says I take after him so, you'll see, one day I'm going to end up probably guarding the crown jewels or something."

The puppy that partly resembled a greyhound grinned and stretched out his front legs lazily. "You talk about protecting something valuable. Well I am going to actually be valuable myself. With my breeding, I'm going to end up the fastest dog ever seen. I am going to win loads of races, and I'll have trophies and then I'll be worth a fortune."

"Well I don't intend to work at all." cut in the little dog, admiring her reflection in the window. "We toy breeds are very popular with famous people. I shall be a celebrity and travel all over the world. I'll be pampered and bought lots of pretty clothes and taken to loads of parties and I won't even have to walk. I'll get carried around in a special bag and the press will follow us and my photograph will be everywhere."

Eventually, each of the puppies had their appointment, said their farewells, and went back to their respective homes. It was some years later, during a walk on the beach, that the three of them found their paths crossing one more time. The German shepherd cross, now huge and powerful, wagged his tail enthusiastically, keen to share his story.

"I live with a wonderful family." he told the others. "We have a big house and a lovely garden to play in. There are four children who are really nicely behaved and I have my own big basket to sleep in."

"So you're just a family dog then?" scoffed the smallest of the three.

The German shepherd smiled. "Last month, two of the older children took me to the beach for walk. I was minding my own business sniffing around at some of the great sticks you find washed up, when I heard one of them cry out. Of course, I was back there like a shot and found a group of nasty boys pushing the children around. Well, instinct took over and I put myself between my family and this gang, snarling at them with my teeth bared. You should have seen them run away!"

"Big deal! Aren't you disappointed? After all, you always said you would be an important guard dog, responsible for expensive jewels."

"Disappointed? How could I be disappointed when I have fulfilled my dreams? You see, I get to protect the most valuable treasure there is – a family that love me."

The little dog snorted, but the other dog nodded eagerly, bouncing on his long legs as he took his turn.

"I understand what you mean about family being the most important thing. I live with a lovely old gentleman on the edge of town. I am his only companion and we used to go for long walks together all over the countryside." A sad look came into the dog's eyes. "He is in hospital at the moment so I am staying here with his sister. But hopefully he will be better soon and then we can go home together."

"Yes that all sounds very sweet, but you're hardly the valuable racer you said you would be." the little dog said mockingly.

The bigger dog just smiled and continued his story.

"A few weeks ago, my owner collapsed while we were out on one of our walks. I was distraught, but I knew what I had to do, and ran off to get help. I have never run so fast in my life. Thankfully we managed to get him to hospital in time. They said had he been left much longer, he would have died."

"But that doesn't exactly make you worth a fortune and nor have you won any trophies."

"Well, actually," the greyhound cross said modestly, "I was awarded a medal by the local community for my heroic actions, but more importantly, my owner said that a dog as dedicated and loyal as me was priceless."

"So what about you then?" The German shepherd cross retorted, somewhat annoyed by the dismissive comments of the toy dog, "You're not exactly hobnobbing with the rich and famous like you claimed you would."

The small dog pawed the ground, slightly embarrassed, but held her head up high as she replied. "Well, you both may have settled for your normal lives, but I haven't given up on my dreams. I'm not going to stick around here forever, you'll see."

Determined to prove herself, and angry with the amused expression on the other dogs' faces, the scruffy Chihuahua cross didn't feel much like returning to her family. After the three dogs had parted company, she sat sulking in a sand dune, ignoring the increasingly plaintive calls of her owner as she searched for her beloved pet. When both the daylight and the sound of her owner's voice began to fade, the little dog's confidence began to waver, but foolish pride kept her hidden until morning.

As the sun rose, she stretched her back and shook the sand from her shaggy coat, a plan to travel to America beginning to form in her mind.

"At least there I will be appreciated." she told herself. "In Hollywood there are loads of celebrities and they will adore me."

And so she set off, taking the streets that she was sure were leading her closer to her destiny, oblivious of the fact that as the day wore on the lanes were becoming more remote, that the traffic was getting scarcer. Just when she felt her paws could not carry her a step further, she found herself in the main high street of an unfamiliar town, and she gazed around, amazed at the dazzling lights that illuminated the shop displays. She trotted over to the nearest window and, putting her paws onto the sill, stared at the array of exciting products and advertising posters, noticing with delight that one even depicted a pretty dog peering proudly out of a designer handbag that was tucked under the arm of an elegant model.

"That will be me soon." she smiled to herself.

Suddenly, she felt herself being scooped up by a pair of large rough hands and stuffed unceremoniously into a dirty holdall. She wrinkled her nose at the unpleasant smell and indignantly scrambled to her feet to try and find the opening so that she could see what was happening. This certainly wasn't how she expected travelling in a bag to feel like. It was bumpy, as if the person carrying her was running, and there were lots of uncomfortable lumpy things, all hard and made of metal that bashed against her. Feeling frightened, she pushed her nose out of the small gap in the zip and started to whine. A hand pushed her back in and a harsh voice growled crossly.

"Keep your noise down you mangy mutt. Someone will hear you."

Not long after the three dogs' meeting on the beach, the young greyhound cross was trotting eagerly along the pavement with his owner.

"Slow down there, speedy!" the old man panted, "I've only just got out of the hospital. I don't want to end up back in there just yet!"

The dog wagged his tail affectionately and started sniffing around a lamppost, allowing his owner to catch his breath. As he was exploring, he heard a sigh and looked up, anxiously. The old man patted his dog lovingly on his head, and smiled sadly.

"Couldn't bear it if you went missing," he indicated a poster that was pinned to the lamp post. "It must be awful losing your dog like that."

Enjoying the affection but not really understanding the reason, the dog moved closer to his owner and looked up at the poster. To his amazement, he saw it had on it a photograph of the dog he had met at the vets, the little dog who wanted to be famous.

"Seems like she disappeared during a walk on the beach," the old man continued, almost to himself, "Don't reckon she'll turn up again – probably dog napped by some unscrupulous person looking to make a quick profit." He shook his head sadly and set off along the pavement.

The dog trotted behind him, looking around inquisitively, although unsure of what his owner was talking about. Then he noticed that the poster wasn't just on the one lamp post. As he continued down the street, he could see that there were the same posters on all the lamp posts, lots more pictures of her, up there for everyone to see.

"Well imagine that!" He thought to himself happily, as he and his owner turned towards home, "It looks like she finally got what she wished for."

Don't Tell Me It's Over

I have often noticed how the graveyards in this area are perched high on the steeply sloping hillsides, the only protection from the grazing sheep being the crumbling dry stone walls. In spite of their apparent isolation from the villages that they serve, I can't help thinking that, with their magnificent views; they would make a lovely final resting place...

* * * * *

The distant clock strikes twelve and the sudden clang pierces the silence of the morning and startles me. Shivering, partly from the feel of the fresh autumn air on my skin, but mostly with anticipation, I wrap my arms more tightly around my chest and stand up for a moment, stamping my feet on the ground, before resuming my usual waiting place, on the bench. Our bench. From here, in the overgrown little grave yard, I can look down over the rows of headstones, soullessly mocking me with their grey toothed grin, and beyond to the quiet sea below. It is beautiful, tranquil, which is why we chose this place.

I glance along the grassy field towards the gap in the wall where he always enters, hoping that I will see him striding towards me, hoping that today he won't be late, but already somehow sensing that he will be. We have been meeting here, on this bench nearly every day, at midday, for just over a year. This is our special place, our special time, when we can be together and all the mundane can be pushed to one side. When, for a brief moment, we can forget the real world and believe in our fantasy.

When we meet, he invariably does all the talking, telling me about his day, his worries and problems, his hopes and dreams. I'm just happy to be with him, to listen, and for a brief moment feel that these plans can somehow include me, that I am, and always will be, a proper part of his life. And sometimes, we just sit in silence together, staring out across the landscape, each of us lost in our own thoughts, our own memories.

Most days he brings me flowers. Sweet peas, when he can get them, and roses. Always pink, always something with a strong scent. He often buries his nose into the soft petals before handing them over, almost as if by doing that, he can purge himself of the rotten stink of his present life, the guilt, the sadness...

The sound of the clock striking quarter past the hour drifts across the air like a sea mist, and I frown, rising again to warm my feet, although my stamping now has more than a little impatience to it. Of course, he has been this late before, rushing up the hillside, his hair more tousled than usual with excuses about meetings that over ran tumbling apologetically between his breathless panting. I smile at the memory and try to reassure myself that today will be the same. But something inside me, call it woman's intuition, senses it is different.

I have always known deep down that we couldn't keep doing this forever, that one day he would stop coming to see me, that he would have to get on with his everyday life, and that I couldn't be a part of it. But for a long while now, I have held onto the fantasy that we would somehow manage. That our relationship would survive against the odds. I know whatever happens I will always love him, and I want to believe that he feels the same. And so I have been trying to ignore the warning signs, small at first, but irritatingly persistent as they nag at my thoughts. The increasingly long silences when he is with me, the covert glances at his watch, and more recently the subtle pause before he casually drops her name into the conversation...

I hear the slam of a car door and turn eagerly, to watch him approach. He seems slower than normal, somehow hesitant, reluctant maybe, and I see him glance nervously behind him as if afraid that he is being watched. Even though I know it is unnecessary, that no one ever comes here except us, I find myself suddenly worrying too, and my eyes automatically scan the stony lay-by on the road below, deserted save for his old car, for signs of someone else. But there is nothing, no one, and I tell myself that I am just being paranoid.

Today he has brought me a single pink rose with a long stem. He doesn't speak at first, but simply stands in front of me and stares down at the flower, his fingers gently brushing the petals, and I watch him carefully, looking for signs that everything is still the same, trying to convince myself that the subtle changes in him are nothing to do with me, with us. Then with a heavy sigh he sits down and begins to talk. He is in the mood to reminisce, and the words tumble out in a waterfall of emotion. Relieved, I sit beside him, and close my eyes to bring the pictures in my mind more clearly into focus. The day we first met, our first kiss, those many stolen moments we shared when we truly believed that we would last forever. I can't help but smile as I relive the memories and open my eyes, turning to him so that I can see the joy in his face too. But then I notice that he has stopped talking and, with a jolt, I see that a single tear is sliding down his cheek. That is when I realize that this is it, the end. That this is going to be goodbye.

He turns again to look back down the hill to his car and I follow his gaze. That's when I see her, leaning against the car bonnet, her hands shoved deeply into her pockets against the cold as she shifts her weight from one foot to another, watching him carefully. He has risen to his feet but makes no move towards her, and I sit, paralyzed, staring at this intruder, my mind pounding with panic. She starts walking towards us, slowly at first, but with a determination to her pace, and I glance at his face. His expression is unreadable.

I don't know what I am expecting, but her calmness surprises me. When she gets near, she stops, says nothing, but simply looks into his eyes with a sad questioning smile. He doesn't respond, and glances down with an almost guilty expression at the single rose, still clutched in his hand as if it shouldn't be there. That is when it hits me. She knows, I think to myself, she knows because he has already told her about us, about me.

After a moment, he begins speaking to me again, but now he is quieter, more hesitant, and I guess it is because he is conscious of her listening. Although I hear the phrases, they are the ones I have been dreading, and so I try to block them out, refusing to accept their inevitability, refusing to believe that he would choose her over me. He finishes by saying that he hopes I will understand. That single word, understand, is like a knife piercing my heart. How can I ever understand? How can I possibly contemplate a future without him, where he doesn't want me? I stare at him, wanting to argue, wanting to grab hold of him, anything to persuade him to change his mind, but I am unable to move or to find the words, and so I am motionless before him, voiceless, powerless.

The silence is broken again by the distant clock striking half past the hour. She takes a tentative step towards him and reaches out, taking his hand, but he resists her gentle tug. Instead, he kneels down, slowly putting the rose to his nose and closing his eyes as he inhales the aroma. His explanation is hesitant but firm. It has been more than a year, it is time for him to move on, and she is...he tails off. His final words of farewell are to reassure me that he won't ever forget me. Then he places a kiss on the petals of the rose and lays it on my grave.

The Bird and the Beast

I have often wondered how ancient legends started – did someone just look at a new landscape and try to make some sense of it? These are stories that have lasted centuries and include wonderful characters, magic, and even morals, and yet no one seems to write them anymore. And so, looking at the unusual shape of Birds' Rock, rising out of the Dysynni Valley, I thought I would try it myself...

* * * * *

A long time ago, when the land was ruled by the beasts, and the sky was ruled by the birds, there was a wide valley. Its ancient hills encircled its grassy plains in a gentle embrace and grey clouds rolled in from the seas marking the rhythm of passing days, seasons and years.

But all was not peaceful in this valley, for there was one beast who wanted to possess the valley for himself. And so each day he would march between the hills, his huge feet shaking the ground, and chase away the other animals that called this land their home. And so there soon came a time when no other creature lived on the floor of that valley. Then the beast turned his face to the skies and saw the birds that flew there and he became jealous.

"This is my valley." he roared, "and you must leave my skies."

But the birds taunted the beast, they flew out of reach of his fists, and at night they would nest high on the hill tops surrounding the valley in secret caves that he could never find. The beast grew more angry; frustrated that he couldn't chase the birds away, and took up rocks from the ground. With the mighty strength in his arms, he hurled them into the skies. And although he had only meant to frighten the birds, one of his rocks hit a small bird and it fell from the sky, landing at the beast's feet. As the small bird lay there, its tears soaked into the ground beneath its head, and its faint song drifted out onto the evening air.

At first, the beast was afraid of what he had done, but seeing how frail the small bird was, he laughed, and began to gather more rocks, meaning to strike the other birds. But as he looked up into the sky, he saw that all the birds had gone.

"I have won!" he declared, "I have conquered all the other beasts and I have conquered all the birds. I am truly the most powerful beast of this land"

But the valley heard the song of the little bird and felt its tears, and the sky turned black with anger. And the words of the little bird's song reached the beasts ears.

"You want to possess this valley, but now the valley will possess you. You will weep for every bird and beast you have chased from the land and from the skies and your tears will be like the rocks you once threw."

And then the ground beneath the beast's feet opened, swallowing first his legs, then his body, until nothing more was left but his mighty head, trapped beside the hills, his face turned towards the skies. His final breath became the mist that creeps along the valley floor in the early morning, and his hair became the tufted grass that clings to the rocky cliffs. Then the little bird flew to the top of his head and began to make a nest so that it could count the tears of the beast. And as the ancient hills encircled the trapped beast and the grey clouds marked the passing years, decades and centuries of his imprisonment, one by one the creatures returned to the valley.

Even after all this time, it is still possible to see the shape of the beast's face trapped in his stony prison. At night, the birds still fly in from the sea to nest on his head, and it is said that every night they count the rocks that lie around him, for these are the tears he has shed.

Waiting to Die

Tucked away amongst the houses and shops of our local town, is a modern single storey building. You wouldn't notice it particularly as you drive past, but every day people come and go, visiting their loved ones with mixed feelings of guilt, sorrow, and fear that one day, it might be their turn...

* * * * *

I couldn't do it. Not the job these nurses do. Every day they come and care for the old folk in this place, always a friendly greeting, always a smile. But behind the smiles and cheeriness they know. I mean, they must know, mustn't they, that everyone here is just biding their time, waiting to die.

Some of them have been waiting for years, getting more frail and more daft with every passing day. And then there are others who come and go in the blink of an eye, almost before they've had time to unpack their belongings. One day they're here, bright as anything, bustling around the day room, offering to help give out the compulsory afternoon cups of tea, and the next, they're being carried out feet first, leaving the nurses and residents shaking their heads with amazement. You see, that's the thing that I've noticed, as I sit here next to my best friend Winnie. You never can tell who is going to be next. It's like God has invented some crazy queuing system that He hasn't explained to anyone. Or maybe it's a heavenly lottery – come on in, Tilly Jones, your number's up.

I once suggested this idea to Winnie, but I don't think she approved. With her strict church upbringing, she always found my irreverence a little shocking, even when we were at school together. But I'm not the only one that thinks it. I know that trying to work out whose turn it is next, if not a strictly acceptable topic of conversation around here, is certainly on most people's minds. You can see it in their eyes, and I would almost swear that Harry, one of the old chaps who sits in the sun lounge, runs a book on it.

Winnie came here a couple of years after me. She had a stroke and never quite recovered enough to go back home. She never married, and so had no children of her own. I know her nephews considered trying look after her, but in the end, they figured that she'd be better off with proper care. I think the fact that my family recommended this place must have helped their decision. So, after a few intense discussions and brave smiles all round, dear old Winnie moved in.

When she first arrived, I worried that she might be one of the quick ones – in and out before the first month's fees had cleared the bank. She was almost too bright, too full of life, to be here. Her plump, rosy face seemed so out of place surrounded by almost skeletal figures, their paper thin skin blotchy with age and disease. But I soon realised it was just an act, a façade she painted on in the morning along with her bright lipstick in order to reassure her family that she was happy, that they had not abandoned her. And although she chatted amiably with her fellow inmates, I could see behind her kind twinkling eyes was a constant dread that one day, she too would be propped up in a wheel chair, a bib tucked into her neckline and some nurse mopping up the drool that slid down her chin as she garbled something unintelligible about having to get the washing done before the children came home from school.

I would watch her sometimes, as she gazed out through the window with dawning realisation that she was now just a spectator in life looking out at the real participants, the people with meaningful lives, while she just watched, waiting for the inevitable. It was on days like that, when the faraway look in her eyes glistened with tears, that I stayed close, praying silently that she would be one of the lucky ones, unexpectedly going in her sleep before the brain rot could begin.

Of course, these thoughts always made me feel a little guilty – was it purely selfishness that made me wish her dead rather than me having to watch her slip away piece by tiny piece? Was it just that I couldn't stand the thought of seeing her merely existing for years as an empty shell, her mind capable only of running confused repeats of the past?

It's not easy slowly losing someone you love. I have seen it in the faces of relatives visiting here. The mixture of repulsion and fear as they pat their loved one reassuringly on the hand and talk about inane topics in overly loud and cheerful tones, whilst inside they are counting the minutes before they can politely leave. It's the occasional visitors that find it the hardest. They are shocked at how living in a place like this can make someone seem to shrink. So they nervously pull up a chair and make polite enquiries as to what the food is like and whether there is anything they need bringing in. Before long, their one sided conversation dries up and their attention is drawn to the television, playing the usual daytime rubbish at a volume too low to really hear. I see them gaze almost glassy eyed at the screen with more attention than it would ever get in their own home. Then, avoiding making eye contact with any of the other residents, they mutter something about going to check if there are enough clean socks, before making a quick dash for the exit, relief at being back out in the real world clearly etched on their faces.

Winnie doesn't get many visitors. Her nephews live a little bit too far away and have lives that are a little bit too busy. It's not that they have forgotten her, but the regular commitment of driving over here has started to wear their patience. I know they try to justify it in their own minds, reassuring themselves that Winnie won't notice if they don't turn up that week, reminding themselves that the nurses are looking after her well, that she is popular with the other residents. To be honest, I don't think Winnie does really notice that they don't come quite so often. And anyway, she's always got me.

We sit together most of the time now, keeping her company in the morning as she slowly chews through her scrambled eggs, enjoying her smiles when someone else's visitor stops briefly at her chair to enquire after her health, then listening to her uneven breathing long into the evening as she dozes fitfully in her armchair. We don't chat. There's no point me saying anything to her, because I know she can't really understand, but I am sure that just sometimes, she knows I'm there, and just sometimes she says something that I know makes sense.

I don't know how long I've been here anymore. Somehow, the days and weeks just merge into a blur. The only things marking the passage of time are the doctor's visits. More pills, different pills, stronger pills...Not that it matters. I've nowhere else to be right now, after all. I like being here with Winnie, and she needs me. So here I am, and here I will stay until...

Increasingly, I find myself thinking about that moment. The moment when she finally goes, when her number comes up on the divine lottery. She's definitely running out of time, that's something

I'm certain of. The odds are stacked against her, and I don't just mean in the book run by Harry in the sun lounge. She's not eating properly any more, and spends a lot more of the day sleeping. I find myself hoping that her nephews will visit again soon, for their own sake rather than hers, before it's too late.

I think she senses it too. You can see it in that faraway look in her eye, as if she is trying to focus on the next life rather than this one. Don't get me wrong, I'm not an expert by any stretch of the imagination, and I don't have any inside knowledge from God or anything. No, it's just a hunch. Something about the sort of questions she asks me late into the night, when she knows I'm listening. Questions about friends of ours, long since departed. The night staff pat her affectionately on her arm, and make bland platitudes, but after they have gone, I try to reassure her as best I can, hoping that she hears me, hoping that the message gets through.

Her nephews finally came yesterday. I think someone here must have telephoned them. They always do that, when they think the end is near. They sat awkwardly beside her bed for an hour, their faces flickering with the many thoughts that must have been rushing through their minds. Neither of them spoke, but then, I'm not sure there was anything they could say. I just kept my distance, let them have a bit of time with her. Afterwards, I heard them standing in the corridor outside, talking to the doctor in hushed tones, and the nurse threw them a shyly sympathetic smile when she brought them tea. There were biscuits too, and relatives only ever get biscuits when someone's on their way out. At least that's what Harry claimed when he lowered the odds on Winnie being next.

And he's right - I don't think her nephews will see her again now. So I'm sitting with her, holding her hand, keeping out of the way every time the nurses come in to check on her. She doesn't open her eyes any more. And her breathing is so quiet, so slow, that you almost think she has stopped. One of the night staff has come in to sit with us. They always do that here. Death watch, they call it. Even though the nurse is just sitting and reading a novel, it's comforting to have her in the room with us, ready and waiting...

Winnie murmurs something, and I squeeze her hand. The nurse looks in our direction briefly, but doesn't get up.

"It's all right Winnie," I say softly, "I'm here."

Well, what else is there to say? That there's nothing to be scared of, that it's not going to hurt, that it's just like drifting off to sleep? Her eyes open slightly and she looks straight at me.

"Tilly...?"

That's when I know. Hearing her say my name like that and knowing she can actually see me sitting here. She smiles and grips my hand.

I lean over so that I can whisper to her. "That's right, Winnie. It's Tilly."

"Is it time?" I think the question is more in her eyes than on her lips, and I know what the answer is, the answer she has been waiting to hear.

"Yes love, it's time for us to go now. I'm here to take you with me. I've been here with you all the time, just waiting for you to die."

Spirits of the Sky

At night we stalk, while children quietly sleep,
In silent stealth, to gather hand in hand.
Along the valley to the banks we keep;
Our arms embrace the dark and marshy land.

      And in the dawn's first light we cast our spell,
      Transforming all around with mystic hue.
      With none but waking crows abroad to tell
      Our whispered secrets form like drops of dew.

As sunlight breaks our hold, away we flee,
The pale gold rays too warm for us to bear,
To higher ground, where we might hide, yet see,
Protected from the morning's brightest glare.

      And here on mountain side, we gather yet,
      Our flowing cloaks cast shadows on the ground
      Where many times before our coven met
      And many times we wait without a sound.

But even now some trespassers draw near
And from our gentle slumber we are torn.
Their ignorance of us is plainly clear
And turns our curiosity to scorn.

        With hasty anger blackening our face,
        We threaten to unleash our furious power
        And down the mountain after them we chase
        And roar as under trees they watch and cower.

In raging torrents, our curses are let loose,
Whipping branches wildly in our wake.
Relentlessly we hurl our worst abuse,
For surely misery is ours to make.

        But quickened tempers often soon recoil;
        Remorseful now, we sit and quietly weep
        Tears of sorrow cleanse the battered soil
        And add to streams and rivers running deep.

Then lightened in our mood we rise again
And, as one, to evening calm we fly
And in the air, now sweet from passing rain,
We link in joyful dance across the sky.

        The setting sun bows to the coming night
        And paints the heavens with a crimson glow.
        Our pink tinged hair streams out in bands of light,
        Reflected in the sea far down below.

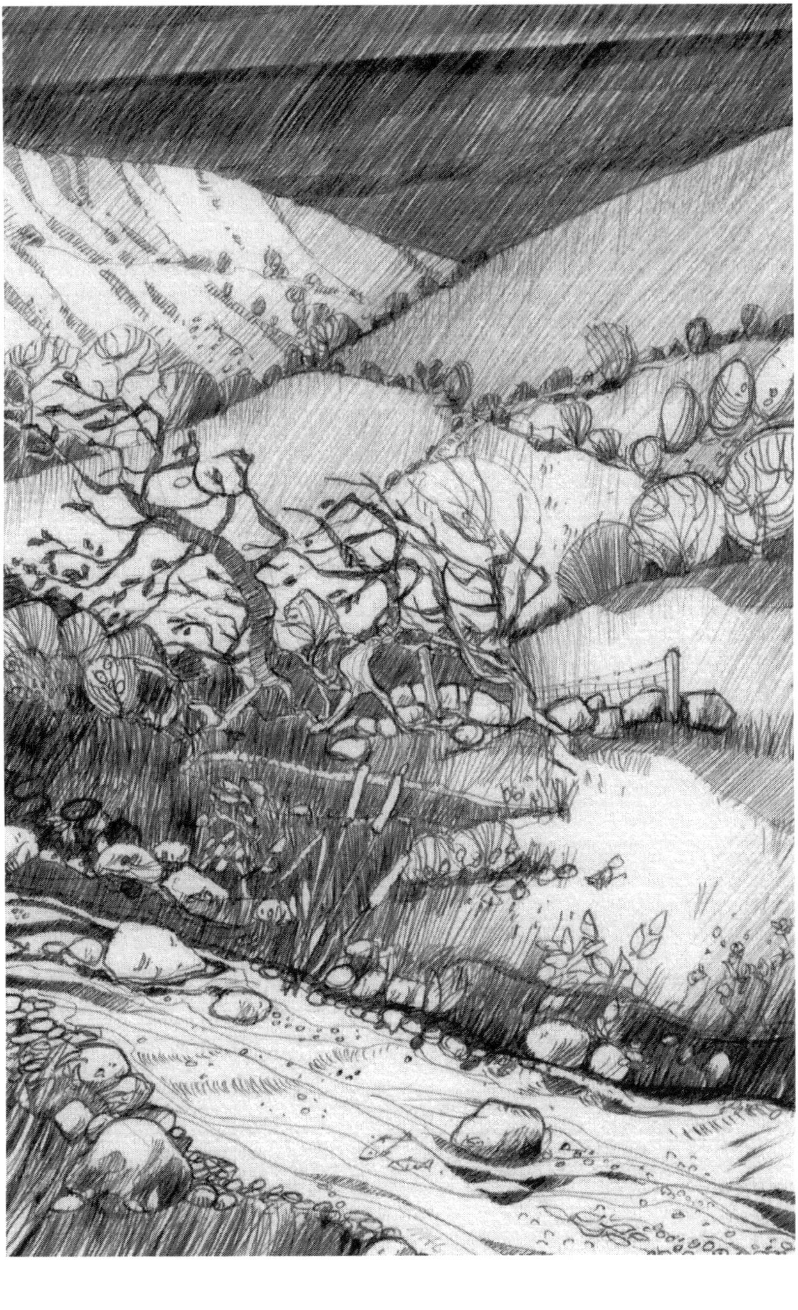

With movement stilled, we huddle against the cold,
Our pale translucence taking solid shape.
Though newly formed, our timeless bodies old,
An endless cycle none of us escape.

        And, as mortals hasten to their bed
        And lonely owls once more take to their flight,
        We create our solid blanket over head
        And cover up the moon and stars from sight.

The Nine Lives of Kitty Carter

A seaside holiday resort looks so different when the tourists go home at the end of the season. It is almost like its life is switched off along with each of the gaudy fairground lights that, over the summer, promised so much excitement and entertainment. It is like a place in limbo, waiting for another season, another life. And all that remains are the left-over fish and chip wrappers, eagerly pounced on by the stray cats...

* * * * *

Bad fish. That was what did it the first time. You see, you have to be so careful with left overs. Kept too long it goes rotten and can cause all types of upset. Well, I was too young and too careless, or more likely just too hungry to care. Living on the streets scrounging food from the waste others throw away is a hard life; take it from one who knows. I was unlucky and got myself a bad dose of food poisoning. So that was that. One life wasted.

Second time around, I was much more cautious. I guess you could say I learnt my lesson, because I avoided fish all together. Not that you will hear people talk about me as cautious. No, I totally got the blame for what happened in that Chinese restaurant, and most unfairly, in my opinion. I didn't start the fire, well, at least not deliberately. Took me by surprise how quickly everything went up in flames, though. Quicker than I could get out, that's for sure.

So onto number three, and I found myself out on the streets again, living on my wits, and the occasional generosity of others. Unfortunately, it turns out that, in search of this generosity, I was, over the years, straying a bit too often into someone else's territory. My actions and my rival caught up with me eventually. What can I say? The fight was short but nasty. I could pretend that he got in a lucky blow, but to be honest, he was bigger and stronger than me, and I didn't really stand a chance.

I guess the fish theme was something that was bound to come back and haunt me, because next I ended up on a little fishing boat. I have to say that it rather suited me. The owner was really friendly and the constant smell of fish is a great cure for sea sickness in my opinion. I quickly learnt the ropes like how to hang on when the waves were tossing the boat like a wild horse, and where to shelter when the rain lashed across the deck. With all that food, friendship and fresh air, I couldn't have been happier. Of course, I've learnt to realise that these things never last. One dark night, a particularly bad storm washed me overboard, and so that was the end of life number four.

I'm not really very proud of what I did next, so you could say I deserved what I got. Maybe I was upset at losing my place on the boat; who knows? But I kind of fell in with the wrong crowd and went a bit wild. We would go out on the streets at night and cause quite a bit of trouble in the neighbourhood. Had a few close shaves, I can tell you. Inevitably, someone always takes things further than you anticipated, and before I knew where I was, there was a fight. And, unfortunately, it was me again, in the wrong place at the wrong time.

Now in contrast, my next life was a cushy number, that's for sure. I got the chance to move into a bed and breakfast establishment, helping out round the place to earn my keep, you know the sort of thing. I was just beginning to feel settled, to think that this was it, and that here I could live out a long and happy life, when fate decided to deal me another blow. After a few funny turns, I was diagnosed as having a tumour. I recall going in for the operation and them giving me the anaesthetic, but after that, nothing.

Apparently those drugs can cause fatal reactions to a handful of unlucky patients, and I guess I was just one of them.

And so there I was, already up to life number seven, and not much to show for it. This time, I managed to get myself living in a nice little flat on the third floor of a swanky new seaside apartment block designed to attract all those city folk wanting a holiday home. Fabulous views from the balcony across the estuary, and with the wind in the right direction, there it was again, that fish theme, this time in the form of a fishy smell that reminded me of my time at sea. And that was my problem - the lure of the balcony. One evening, I leant just a little bit too far and, well three floors up its going to hurt, isn't it?

After that, I thought I would try staying much closer to the ground. Ok, so it seemed like a good idea at the time, but a slight lapse in concentration while crossing the road and suddenly it's all over. I don't think the driver even stopped after he hit me, but then, I wasn't really in any fit state to notice.

So now, by my reckoning, I'm on my ninth life. And so far, as they say, so good. I have managed to reach a ripe old age and certainly learnt some lessons along the way which is all I think anyone can expect. And I have also tried to make it a good life, you know the sort of thing, helping others, sharing when I can. But now as I find myself growing old, I increasingly wonder what will come next. My joints are aching and stiff with old age, and my heart is heavy with the memories of the many friends I have lost over the years. I can't help feeling like I would just like a nice long rest. But I guess we don't get a choice in these things. This karma thing is quite complex, and as far as I can tell from my own experience, the whole business of reincarnation is pretty unpredictable. When I look back at the different lives I have lived, the different people I have been... Still, you never know, maybe next time, if there is a next time, I might even get to come back as a cat.

Ticking,
Time rings a
Tree.

Contents of Illustrations

Winter Grazing	3
Old Cottage	10
Old Room	15
Hanging Oaks	18
Woodland Glade	21
Winding Road	24
Beach House	26
Seaside	35
High Street	38
Shaded Bench	43
Headstone	46
Birds' Rock	48
Coastal Path	49
Hillside Farm	53
Forest Walk	56
Mountain Stream	61
Solitary Boat	64
The Graveyard	68